Pipi and Pou Review

It's [the] wry humour from the characters that makes this book so entertaining. Pipi and Pou are well-rounded characters who, despite their superhero abilities, still feel like real kids with their own problems and priorities: 'They loved being superheroes. It was just that sometimes they wanted to relax, to be lazy, to read a book, play on screens, watch television,' Tipene writes. The depth of the characters made these books spring to life from the page.

Pipi and Pou show us that we don't need supernatural abilities to be kaitiaki for the environment, and that protecting the natural world is rewarding, community-building, and fun. These books are sure to be a hit with kids and adults alike. I'm looking forward to seeing what more adventures this trio of kaitiaki get up to.

- **Hannah Marshall** *(The Sapling)*

Recipient of a 2022 Contestable Fund Grant from Copyright Licensing New Zealand

Produced with the support of:

First published by OneTree House Ltd, New Zealand, 2023

Text © Tim Tipene, 2023
Illustrations © Isobel Te Aho-White, 2023

9781990035296

All rights reserved. No part of this publication may be reproduced, stored in a retrieval system or transmitted in any form or by any means, electronic, mechanical, photocopying, recording or otherwise, without the prior permission of the publisher.

Printed in New Zealand, YourBooks

10 9 8 7 6 5 4 3 2 1   3 4 5 6 7 / 2

and the
100 LEGS OF TERROR

Tim Tipene

illustrated by
Isobel Te Aho-White

KAITIAKI

Guardians and Protectors of the natural world.

NANA

A kuia and a tohunga, an expert in the natural world, who holds experience and wisdom. She leads and guides her mokopuna, Pipi and Pou, through their adventures in being kaitiaki.

Nana is also a master chef.

PIPI

When she runs, she flies.
She likes to win and
she loves to sing.
With the words, 'Pouākai,
haere mai!', Pipi transforms
into a Pouākai, a giant eagle.
Along with her cousin, Pou, Pipi
assists her grandmother, Nana, in
caring for and protecting the natural
world.

POU

A keen rugby player who also loves
being in water and coming first
against his cousin.
He is mighty. He is fierce.
When Pou cries, 'Taniwha, kia kaha!',
he changes into a Taniwha.
Like Pipi and Nana, Pou is a
superhero for the environment.

Tahi

Pipi and Pou could hear Nana speaking in the backyard.

'Who's she talking to now?' Pipi groaned, heading out the door to investigate.

Her grandmother was often communicating with some being or entity from the natural world, and such conversations tended to lead the whānau off on another life-threatening adventure.

'It's probably the wind telling her stuff

again,' guessed Pou, following his cousin. 'Or some insect.'

'Shh,' Nana whispered to her moko when they reached the garden. 'I'm on a call.'

She pointed to the cell phone pressed against her ear.

Pipi and Pou shared a glance. Finding their grandmother conversing with an actual person was the last thing that they had been expecting.

'Mōrena ... can you hear me!' Nana said loudly.

Frowning, she lifted the device up in front of her face and peered at it through her glasses. She was watching for bars of coverage on the screen.

'There's no reception,' she grumbled, returning the phone to the side of her head. 'Tēnā koe ... are you there?'

Nana moved around on the lawn trying to locate a spot where the line was clearer. In the corner of the garden, she balanced on her left leg and extended her right leg and arm straight behind her. Using her left hand, she raised the phone into the air and leaned forward.

'Kia ora!' she cried.

'Check that out!' muttered Pou, gapping at his grandmother's mad-as posturing skills. 'Is that a yoga or a dance pose?'

'I'm pretty sure it's ballet,' Pipi replied, looking dumbfounded. 'They call it an arabesque.'

Thinking elevation might help with the connection, Nana stepped up onto a chair that was next to the garage. When this didn't work, she proceeded to go even higher, onto an old, retired barbecue that she had turned into her garden workbench.

'Ata mārie!' she called into the phone.

There was still no reception so Nana proceeded to climb the wooden trellis that was leaning against the side of the garage. The second-hand framework had been a gift from Uncle Hēmi, and Nana was planning to use it to support the tomatoes and beans she intended to grow this year.

'Nana, be careful!' Pipi urged as she walked over. 'That fencing doesn't look very strong.'

The tohunga scaled the trellis and pulled herself up onto the garage roof.

The two cousins stood underneath peering upwards.

'Far out, Nan,' said Pou, shaking his head

while keeping his eyes on her. 'I hope you're not expecting us to catch you if you fall. I'm not saying that you're heavy or anything, it's just that I'd have to be a taniwha to stop you from hitting the dirt.'

'That's not the point,' Pipi tutted. 'She shouldn't be doing it at all!' With her hands fixed firmly on her hips, she glared at their grandmother. 'What are you thinking? Get down from there you crazy old woman, before you get hurt!'

Nana held out the device and shrugged. 'But I don't know who it is that is trying to reach me. No name is showing and I can't hear them.'

She walked about on top of the garage attempting to increase the phone's coverage.

'They can call back if it's important!' stressed Pipi. 'It's not worth you ending up in hospital!'

Nana pointed at the horizon. 'Oh, what's that?'

Pipi and Pou spun around simultaneously; however, apart from the usual view from their home, of the ocean between forest-covered hills and a cloudy blue sky in the background, there was nothing to see. When the pair turned back, they found that Nana had gone from the garage up onto the roof of the house.

'Whoa, what!' Pou gasped, stepping backward. 'No way! How did she do that? That's like a three-metre jump.'

'Nana!' Pipi yelled.

'Tēnā koe ...' they heard her say into the phone.

Pou looked at Pipi while gesturing at their grandmother. 'She's a Ninja.'

Nana appeared at the edge of the whare. 'Āe,

this is Nana. He aha, what do you want? Kia ora ... are you still there? Can you hear me?'

She held onto an old television aerial and leaned off the side of the roof, over the driveway.

'That's better,' she smiled. 'The line's much clearer now.'

'Ha-ha,' Pou laughed. 'Check it out, our gran is a Kung Fu master.'

Pipi's face was full of thunder.

'OMG!' she growled, staring up at Nana. 'If it were Pou or I taking risks like that you would be telling us off! Some great role model you are!'

Pipi's reprimanding of her grandmother was interrupted by a black, electric SUV with tinted windows that pulled into the driveway. Nana and her moko paused to watch the male driver and the female front passenger climb out. The pair's physiques were muscular in their dark suits and they wore shades, and had mics in their ears, like special agents. The pair of bodyguards stood tall, surveying the area. Certain that the coast was clear of any danger or prying eyes, the driver opened the back door of the vehicle, allowing a second woman to emerge. She was in her thirties and was also dressed in a black suit; however, her jacket glittered with a faint silvery koru design. Her silky black locks were tied back, with two large, white-tipped, black huia feathers standing upright, forming a V shape above her head. They gave the slightly built woman a chiefly appearance. As did the greenstone pendants that dangled from each of her ears. Like Nana, she had a moko kauae, a chin tattoo, and also like Nana, she was holding a phone to her ear.

Pou nudged Pipi. 'Look who it is.'

'No way,' she mumbled. 'It can't be.'

The woman's high heels click-clacked on the concrete driveway.

'E, Nan, tēnā koe,' she said, looking up at the tohunga still on the roof, hanging from the television aerial. 'It was me on the line.'

'Auē, Prime Minister Reihana,' Nana exclaimed as she eyed the stained track pants and ragged hooded top she was wearing. These were her gardening clothes. Her 'rags' she called them. Not what the elder would want the political leader of Aotearoa to see her in.

'I wished you had called first,' Nana grumped as she headed back to the trellis. 'I would have prepared ... some kai.'

16

'I was trying to,' the minister beamed, waving her device. 'There is a matter of the utmost importance that I need to discuss with you.'

Rua

Pipi fetched the ladder from the garage and, together with Pou, she propped it up against the side of the whare before Nana could reach the trellis.

Prime Minister Reihana and her bodyguards watched the tohunga climb down from the roof while her mokopuna held the ladder and offered instructions.

'You're certainly looking fit and well, Nan,' Minister Reihana observed once she'd reached the ground. 'You wouldn't catch my mother hanging off the side of a house like that.'

Nana smiled. 'It's my Rongoā, dear. It keeps me going.'

'I could probably do with some of that traditional Māori medicine,' remarked the minister. 'To help me get through all my meetings and parliament speeches.'

Nana gave her hongi, a kiss on the cheek and a hug.

The prime minister responded with a grin, closing her eyes and relishing the older women's squeeze. 'So good to see you. It's been too long.'

'Well, you've been busy running the country,' Nana noted. 'Visiting whānau and friends wouldn't be easy with your hectic schedule.'

The tohunga welcomed the bodyguards, Māka and Kirihi, in the same manner that she had the prime minister.

Pipi and Pou felt their cheeks burn when Minister Reihana greeted them. Having the leader of Aotearoa randomly turn up at their home had rendered them both speechless.

Pipi bowed.

'Tēnā koe, your highness,' she said, finally finding her words.

Pou copied her.

Minister Reihana chuckled and gently poked Pipi in the ribs with her finger to make the girl smile and relax. 'Kāo, I'm no highness. While I believe that every woman is a queen, I'm no ruler. I'm a democratically elected representative of the people.' She bowed back to the two cousins, then grabbed them, one after the other, embraced them, and kissed their cheeks.

Nana started to head into the whare.

'Put the jug on, Pou,' she instructed. 'We'll have a cup of tea to go with the cheese scones I made this morning. Pipi, you can open a jar of my Blackberry Jam.' Nana smiled proudly at the manuhiri and tapped the side of her nose with her forefinger. 'I have my secret blackberry patches. My moko help me pick them when they're ripe.'

The prime minister raised her hands.

'Taihoa, Nan,' she insisted. 'We'll have to do that another time. I'm here this morning because the country needs your help.'

The tohunga and her mokopuna faced a now serious Minister Reihana.

21

'A rāhui was placed on a ngahere, a forest on the west coast,' the minister explained. 'It was to protect one of our eldest and most sacred of kauri trees, Tīkokekoke.'

'He rangatira,' Nana acknowledged, knowing of the old rākau.

'I read about that tree at school,' said Pou.

'Āe tika, it's been in the news,' Minister Reihana continued. 'All of our kauri have been under threat of disease, yet there is something else going on with Tīkokekoke. I sent scientists into the ngahere to conduct tests on him, only to have them come running out full of fear. In response, police entered the forest to investigate and after a day even they ran scared. They claimed that there was some sort of monster stalking them.'

'Aiii,' Nana breathed with a furrowed brow.

'Ha, I know right? A monster, who would believe it?' laughed the minister. 'Our country is known for taniwha. Every area has their stories, but an actual, physical horror walking around in broad daylight? I don't think so.'

Pipi and Pou looked at one another. They had seen plenty of monsters on their adventures with Nana.

Minister Reihana sighed. 'You imagine what would happen if the government announced publicly that there was a monster in one of our forests. First people would think that I was pulling their leg, and then, when they realised that I wasn't, they would panic.'

'Are they sure that it was a monster?' Nana asked, her fingers running over the grooves of her moko kauae.

The prime minister shook her head, 'No one got a good look at the thing, of course. It was probably just a shadow, or someone pulling a prank to scare others away. I was going to send in the armed forces to secure the area, but the local kaumātua and kuia requested that I ask you to come and have a look first. Nan, you have quite the reputation among our people for bringing peace to communities.'

'Oh,' the tohunga muttered, looking down at her feet. Nana never liked it when people made a fuss about her and her mahi. She preferred staying humble.

'So will you take a look?' Minister Reihana pleaded.

Nana nodded. 'Āe, my moko and I will visit Tīkokekoke.'

Prime Minister Reihana looked perplexed. 'You're taking the kids with you? E, Nan, I don't believe that there's an actual monster, but that ngahere is pretty wild. I can organise a babysitter for Pipi and Pou.'

The cousins both glared at the minister.

'Babysitter?' Pipi tutted.

'I can also send some professionals to help you find your way through the forest,' the minister offered.

'Kāo, me and my moko will be fine,' answered Nana.

Toru

Prime Minister Reihana was concerned that Nana was not accepting her offer of child care and a guide, but there was no arguing with the kuia. Nana knows best, so the leader and her security officers left in their black SUV.

Shortly after, Nana and her moko climbed into their old car, Betsy.

'Stay home with a babysitter!' Pipi spat. 'I'm a pouākai, Pou's a taniwha!'

The girl was so annoyed with the prime

minister's suggestion that she and her cousin remain behind with a minder, that she started doing a haka in the front passenger seat.

Betsy usually runs on waiata, but with Pipi's haka the car's engine roared to life.

'Whoa, sounds like there's a turbo under the hood today, Nana,' Pou laughed from the back.

'Just as well,' Nana remarked, with both of her hands gripping the steering wheel. 'Considering what Minister Reihana was saying we've no time to lose. We need to get to that ngahere.'

She directed the car out of the driveway, and with a cough and splutter emitting from the motor the whānau headed off up the road.

Pou leaned back and eyed the white and grey clouds in the sky.

'Is the prime minister married?' he queried.

Nana looked at him in the rearview mirror. Pipi stopped her haka abruptly and spun about.

'You've got to be kidding me!' she sneered.

Pou shrugged. 'What?'

'She's a bit old for you, don't you think?' challenged Pipi.

'I just asked?' he argued. 'Anyway, I'm not going to be a kid forever. I could marry her when I grow up.'

Nana chuckled and watched the road in front.

Pipi screwed up her face. 'Did you bump your head?'

Pou didn't know what all the fuss was about. 'What's wrong with Prime Minister Reihana? She's clever, intelligent, a leader, a real wahine toa.' He gave a silly grin. 'She's beautiful in every way.'

Pipi turned back around. 'Yeah, okay, Reihana's an awesome woman, but remember that she wanted us to stay home with a babysitter. That's probably what she'll do to you if you marry her.'

Nana shook with laughter. She was finding her grandchildren's conversation very amusing.

'Whatever,' Pou tutted, pushing his cousin's seat with his foot.

'I would rather be like Kirihi,' Pipi continued. 'A bodyguard. I bet she's a well-trained assassin, ready to take out anyone.' Pipi karate chopped the air. 'She promised to show me her firearm one day.'

'Dream on,' Pou smarted, returning his gaze to the clouds above.

'Me, a dreamer? I'm not the one who's got a

crush on the Prime Minister of Aotearoa,' Pipi stated, ensuring that she had the last say.

Nana smiled softly. 'I think you should both keep aspiring to achieve whatever it is you want, my moko,' she encouraged. 'Think big.'

The whānau drove through the day and into the night, eventually stopping in a small town to rest. Then early the next morning they set off again, travelling for several more hours before they reached the forest. Nana finally brought her waka to a halt in an empty car park on the edge of the ngahere. Her door creaked as she pushed it open and stepped out.

'Ahh, smell that fresh air,' the tohunga breathed.

Pipi and Pou joined her outside. 'At least it's not too hot,' Pou sighed, scanning the dense bush around them.

'Perfect weather for a walk.' Nana observed, eyeing the overcast sky. She put her left forearm through the straps of her woven flax kete and leaned on her carved tokotoko.

Pipi stood with her hands on her hips studying the native forest with its multi shades of green and chorus of bird song. 'So, the scientists and the police reckon that there is a monster somewhere in this ngahere. What do you think, Nan?'

'Well, if there is, we'll know soon enough,' she replied.

The cousins watched her head off into the trees before falling into line behind her.

'I can't see a track anywhere,' Pou cautioned, showing concern. 'How do we know which direction to take?'

'The trees will tell me the way,' said the tohunga, without looking back.

Pipi and Pou turned to one another. They had been on many escapades with Nan, and if there was one thing they had learnt it was that things rarely went to plan.

'Best to stay alert,' Pou warned quietly.

'Āe, be ready to change,' agreed Pipi.

They continued after their grandmother in silence, each scouring the bush around them.

The whānau walked for an hour before a giant kauri started to come into view.

'See, I told you the rākau would tell me how to get to him,' Nana proclaimed, extending an arm and opening her hand to present Tīkokekoke in the ngahere ahead.

The cousins gaped at the enormous kauri as

they made their way through the undergrowth towards him.

Tīkokekoke was clearly the rangatira of this forest, with his crown of branches towering over all the other trees. Beneath his canopy of cascading green leaves, a selection of other plants could be seen perched atop his limbs, forming a garden in the sky that was well beyond the reach of the ground far below. The kauri was the biggest in every way, with his incredibly wide, light grey trunk standing grand and dwarfing all the life surrounding it.

'Wow, he must be like two thousand years old,' Pou blurted, unable to see the top of the tree through the foliage of the other rākau as he walked.

'Much older,' said Nana.

She bowed to the ancient Tīkokekoke. 'E te rangatira, tēnā koe.'

'It would take like twenty people or more to circle his trunk,' Pipi said with awe.

The closer he got, the more Pou tried to peer through the roof of the forest, in search of the peak of the kauri. 'I think he's touching the clouds.'

The boy was looking up so much that he wasn't watching where he was going and almost tripped over a fallen branch.

'Mind your step,' Nana advised.

Together the tohunga and her mokopuna continued to venture nearer and were only metres from the base of Tīkokekoke when suddenly the ground beneath their feet gave way. It happened so fast that the whānau had no chance to stop themselves from falling.

'Argh!' they cried as they dropped into a deep, dark hole.

Whā

Nana, Pipi and Pou had fallen into a large hole and it didn't end there. When they hit the dirt, they started tumbling and sliding down a steep incline that led to a large underground tunnel. The further the trio slid, the darker it got.

'Uh ... what's ... happening?' shouted Pipi as she bounced along, before tumbling head over heels.

'I can't see!' Pou yelled.

The dirt under them disappeared again and

they dropped several feet further before landing with a thud.

'Ow!' Nana groaned.

'You alright, Nan?' Pou asked, jumping to his feet and reaching out for her in the dark.

'Kāo!' Nana snapped. 'My knee, my hip, my nono, I'm sore everywhere!'

'I've got you,' he responded, his hands grabbing a hold.

'Hey, let go!' Pipi demanded, pushing him off. 'I'm not Nana!'

'I didn't know!' Pou argued. 'How could I, it's pitch black in here.'

'Where are we?' Pipi questioned, brushing her clothes off with her hands. She couldn't see the dirt, but she was certain that she could feel it all over her. The girl peered around trying to make sense of the darkness. 'Our voices are echoing. We must be in some sort of cave.'

'The last thing I saw before it went black was a tunnel,' noted Pou. 'We fell into it and now we're deep in the ground.'

'Weird,' Pipi remarked. 'What would a tunnel be doing here? And who made it?'

The cousins felt Nana's hand latch onto them.

'Shhh, whakarongo, you two,' she hushed. 'What's that noise?'

Pipi and Pou froze like statues and listened intently.

'It sounds like scratching,' suggested Pipi. 'Whatever it is, it's getting louder.'

'Could it be bugs?' Pou queried. 'Like a whole lot of them heading this way? I'm hearing a hundred legs at least.'

'Eww, don't say that,' shuddered Nana. 'Makes my skin crawl.'

Pipi and Pou both shivered at the idea of insects creeping all over them.

The noise increased, surrounding the family.

'Guys, I don't think we want to stick around to find out what that sound is,' Pipi stated.

'Nan, there's a light on your phone,' Pou suddenly remembered. 'Turn it on.'

'Really?' frowned the tohunga. 'A light on my phone? Are you sure? I never knew that.'

'Auē, this new technology, eh, Nan?' Pipi joked. 'You just can't keep up.'

'Āe, that's exactly what I say,' the old woman agreed.

Scratch, scratch, scratch, the grating noise continued.

'Where's the phone?' Pou asked, tracking Nana's voice in the dark.

'How should I know, I dropped my kete,' she explained. 'I managed to keep a hold of it all through the tunnel until that last fall.'

Pipi got down on her hands and knees, and fumbled in the blackness, blindly feeling her way over the cold, damp ground.

'You know, we wouldn't be in this situation if Pou and I both had our own phones,' she took the opportunity to point out. She had been on at Nana for some time now, hankering after a mobile. She would show her adverts offering discounts on the television, or on billboards, but her grandmother would usually counter with, 'We don't have the money,' or 'Young people didn't walk around with phones in my day, and we grew up just fine.'

Today her response was, 'You have your Chromebooks for kura. That's all you need for now.'

'That's all you need for now,' Pipi quietly mimicked, with a curled-up lip.

'He aha?' Nana queried.

'Nothing.'

SCRATCH, SCRATCH, SCRATCH!

Pipi picked up the pace of her search.

'I found your kete,' she announced triumphantly.

'Ka pai!' cheered the tohunga.

'It's empty,' the girl moaned.

Nana tutted. 'That's no good.'

'Your stuff must be all over the place,' Pipi informed her. She continued casting around the cavern floor and finally ... 'I think I've got it.'

With a click, the phone's screen lit up.

Nana located her glasses on the end of the cord dangling from around her neck. She wiped the dirt from the specs and put them on.

'Hika mā! Auē, things are just getting worse,' she sighed.

Pou placed a hand on her shoulder. 'What is it?'

'There's a crack in one of my lenses,' she explained. 'I'll have to get it fixed when we're back home. At least it hasn't fallen out.'

Using the faint glow emitting from the phone the tohunga started to gather her belongings from the ground.

'How big is this place?' Pipi questioned. 'I can't even see the roof.'

SCRATCH, SCRATCH, SCRATCH!

'Turn on the torch light,' Pou directed, trying to take the device from Pipi.

'I can do it!' she growled, pulling it back from him.

A sudden brightness burst from the rear of the phone.

'There we go,' Pipi smiled.

The sound of jaws moving made Nana, Pipi and Pou look up.

Bearing down above them was the huge, dark brown head of a gigantic, female hura, (centipede). Her head alone was almost the size of Nana's car. The hura had pincer-like forcipule claws that extended from either side of her first segment and curved around to frame her face. Her claws were opened outwards to reveal sharp mandible jaws with long strands of saliva trailing to her extended antennae, which were reaching down towards the three quivering humans.

The light also revealed the enormous brown segmented exoskeleton of the centipede that was now coiled around the whānau several times. There was a multitude of bright yellow, jointed legs that had been the source of the scratching noises. The limbs were set in pairs, two sticking out from each segment, and every one of them had a black pointed hook on the end.

'Oh,' Nana gasped at the sight of the behemoth.

'I think we've found our monster,' muttered Pipi moving closer to her grandmother.

It was then that she dropped the phone and the light switched off, returning the cave to complete blackness.

'I would just like to point out that those claws on either side of the hura's head are poisonous,' mentioned Pou, having studied elongated myriapods at school. 'And she doesn't need eyes to see. Centipedes are excellent hunters in the dark.'

Rima

Pipi sprung into the air.

'Pouākai, haere mai!' she roared, pulling a mighty pūkana.

There was a flash of light and Pipi changed into a pouākai, a giant eagle.

The dazzling flare caused Hura to rear backward.

Pipi Pouākai flew up, but with the cave plunged back into darkness again she couldn't see where she was going, and flew head–first into the roof.

'Ouch!' she cried, flapping about. 'We're useless if we can't see!'

With her talons the eagle clung to the ceiling,

retracted her wings, and froze, hanging upside down. She could sense danger in the blackness, advancing towards her. Her commotion had caught the attention of the hura. The gigantic centipede was now above them, crawling over the roof, a predator hunting for its prey. Her movements caused specks of dirt to drop.

Beneath and unaware of the creature's precise location, Pou brushed the falling debris from his hair.

'In te reo Māori the giant centipede of Aotearoa is called hura,' he whispered, reciting his learning. 'But, in this case, I will call her Hurahura. Some sources say that they can grow to 20 centimetres long, while others say 25 centimetres. They are quite rare these days because introduced rats have devastated their numbers. I never read of a gigantic hura though. Any ideas on how to handle this, Nan?'

The tohunga raised her head. Taking a deep breath, she began to sing an old waiata. Her voice filled the cave and small glows began to appear all over the roof in response.

'Titiwai,' chirped Pipi Pouākai.

Nana continued to sing and the light from the glow-worms grew in intensity, lighting up the darkness.

'Kia pai mai hoki! Ka rawe, Nan!' Pou applauded. 'Finally, we have vision.'

The surroundings were looking less like a cave and more like a candlelit chamber thanks to the sparks of titiwai. The whānau could now see the details of where they were and what was going on around them. They appeared to be in a large, central burrow with three tunnels leading off, including the one above, which they had fallen through. Large tree roots protruded from the dirt roof and walls and ran into the floor. These were the roots of Tīkokekoke.

Hurahura, the gigantic centipede, had built a nest beneath the great kauri, and Nana and her moko had dropped into it like a home delivery meal. The long myriapod was looped multiple times around the whānau, her body covering much of the floor, the walls, and even parts of the ceiling.

Pou eyed his cousin, Pipi Pouākai, clutching the roof overhead.

Hurahura had lost interest in the raptor. Her focus had now shifted to the boy and old woman moving about below. With her

front limbs no longer gripping the top of the borrow, she reached for the ground. Each of her movements caused a chain of adjustments that rippled through her entire body so that every segment and leg repositioned in support of her direction. Once down, Hurahura reared her head like a snake preparing to strike. Her front legs scratched at the air while her black-tipped, pincer-like claws and sharp mandibles were opening and closing in anticipation of a fresh, tasty kill. She reached out with her antennae, feeling for Pou and Nana.

'Get off me!' Pou yelled, pushing the long feelers away.

Hurahura reared again and a glob of saliva fell from her jaws, splatting on his face.

'Yuck,' Pou groaned, wiping the slimy goo

from his sight. 'That's disgusting.'

'Pou, watch out!' squawked Pipi Pouākai from overhead.

Hurahura had lunged with lightning speed, snapping at Nana and Pou with her venomous claws. While Pou dived forward to evade her grasp, Nana fell backward, landing on her butt.

'Ow, not my nono again,' she cringed.

It was apparent to the tohunga that she was going to have a number of souvenirs in the form of bruises from this adventure.

Having been close to catching the woman and the boy, Hurahura hurriedly weaved from left to right, sending waves through her body, while her antennae scoured the ground searching for the pair.

Dodging the legion of legs, Nana grabbed her

kete and tokotoko, and crawled beneath some of Tīkokekoke's roots to hide.

Pou was now constantly in motion, dashing all over the place to avoid detection from the centipede's feelers.

'Her eyesight is poor,' he continued spouting his lesson on centipedes. 'They only register light and dark. She mostly sees by touch and smell.'

Nana peered out from her spot of concealment. The knuckles on her hands were white from gripping the tree roots so hard.

'Hey, Mr Zoologist, stop the gasbagging and just get out of there!' she commanded.

Hurahura was now fixed on Pou's movements.

'She can feel your vibrations,' Pipi Pouākai called from the roof.

The centipede was closing in on the boy.

Pou slapped his thighs and stomped his foot.

'Taniwha, kia kaha!' he roared, pulling a mighty pūkana.

There was a flash of light and Pou turned into a taniwha, a monster.

Hurahura wasn't startled by the flare this time.

'Watch out!' cried Pipi Pouākai. 'She's going to strike!'

'Pou!' yelled Nana.

Ono

In the glow-worm-lit cave the taniwha stood directly in front of the giant centipede. He placed his feet firmly in the ground, feeling the dirt between his toes. Hurahura thrust at him with her toxic fangs.

'Taniwha Tackle!' Pou te Taniwha thundered.

With lightning speed, he grabbed one claw with his left hand and the other claw with his right and held on. He could see venom dripping from the black tips of the dagger-like prongs.

Hurahura attempted to pull back and free her

pincers. When that didn't work she retracted her claws, drawing the taniwha closer and extending her mandibles forward to try and bite him. He leaned away from the snapping jaws and gripped the claws even tighter to keep a space between them.

Bending her body beneath her, the centipede reached out with her legs to hook onto him. She was planning to use her limbs to pull the little monster into her mouth. Seeing this, Pou te Taniwha released his grip on the centipede, which sent both of them stumbling backward.

Hurahura hissed and shook her head. She rolled the ends of her antennae inwards and calmly ran each one individually through her jaws to clean them off. Her attention then returned to the hunt and the taniwha that she now had lined up directly in front of her.

Pou te Taniwha looked about. He had
been so busy focusing on Hurahura's head
and pincers that he hadn't noticed her body
creeping in. The gap in the centre of the coiled
centipede had gotten smaller. Hurahura had
him surrounded and he couldn't see any way to
escape. He was trapped.

'C'mon tama, you can do it!' urged Nana, from
within the roots of Tīkokekoke. 'Don't give up!'

Pipi Pouākai had been studying the gigantic
myriapod from the ceiling above. 'The safest
place is on top of her, just behind her claws.'

'You're kidding, right?' frowned Pou the
monster, without taking his eyes off Hurahura.

'Pipi, you can't be serious?' Nana exclaimed.

'Think about it,' the eagle argued. 'It's the
only place where she can't grab him.'

Pou te Taniwha watched the giant centipede getting ready to strike at him for the third time. Her dripping claws and jaws kept opening and closing. If there was one thing that Pou had learnt about hura from school it was that they are ferocious and highly effective hunters; assassins of the insect world. Typically, they are much smaller though, and only hunt spiders and other insects. Being a giant meant that Hurahura preyed on bigger animals, which put Pou and his family on her menu.

Pou te Taniwha thought about his life. There was so much more that he wanted to do. He didn't want to die like this. Suddenly a thought came to him.

'It's just like playing rugby,' he told himself. 'I've got the ball and she's out to tackle me.'

With that in mind Pou te Taniwha ran straight

for Hurahura's jaws. With her fangs spread wide, she lunged.

Nana tapped her tokotoko against the roots of Tīkokekoke, distracting and putting the centipede off her attack. Pipi Pouākai flapped her wings and squawked to do the same. Pou te Taniwha did a dummy step which further confused Hurahura and enabled him to evade her bite. Then the taniwha sprung up, over her legs, and onto her armoured back where he ran along the segments towards her head as though he was running down a field toward the try line. Hurahura was fast as she curled around in pursuit of him, but today the monster was faster.

'Taniwha Tackle!' he yelled, leaping onto the first section from where her forcipule claws protruded. 'Score!'

Pou te taniwha pressed himself against the hard exoskeleton and gripped on for dear life with his hands and feet. The antennae of Hurahura turned back and found him, feeling all about his face. She tried to reach overhead with her claws and mandibles to pierce his skin and grab a hold, however, just as Pipi Pouākai had predicted, the myriapod couldn't reach.

Hurahura became enraged. Her tail rolled over and up into the air like the sting of a scorpion, where it bore down on Pou te Taniwha. She stabbed and prodded at his tough skin with the sharp hooks of her tail legs, attempting to pull him off.

'Argh!' Pou grimaced, but he wouldn't budge.

Hurahura writhed, turning, twisting, and contorting her body. She sent circles in waves that ran the length of her being, taking rear segments over her head in an attempt to knock the rider off, or better still to push him forward to her toxic daggers. Pou te Taniwha held on firmly. He eyed the many legs reaching out for him as they went by.

Meanwhile, Hurahura's vigorous movement caused the whole cave to shake and rocks to fall. Pipi Pouākai had to let go of the roof and flutter about in the air to stay clear of the gigantic centipede.

Worried for her grandson, Nana crawled out from under the tree roots. Placing a kōauau pongāihu, a small gourd nose flute, to her nostril, she breathed life into it. The delicate tone of the wind instrument filled the cave and drew the attention of Hurahura. The myriapod became still and quiet.

'Careful, Nan,' warned Pipi Pouākai as she settled on a ledge nearby. 'She's probably tracking you now.'

Opening her throat, Nana gave an almighty karanga, calling to Hurahura. She told the giant centipede who she was, and where she had come from. The tohunga informed the creature that the giant eagle and the taniwha were her mokopuna, and that as a whānau they had come in peace.

'We are kaitiaki!' sang Nana. 'Guardians and protectors of the natural world!'

Hurahura reached back with her antennae, rubbing them all over Pou te Taniwha's forehead, cheeks, and nose once more. It was now his turn to wriggle.

'Uh c'mon!' he yelled. 'Not again. That's gross.'

As uncomfortable as it was, the taniwha refused to release his hold.

'That's why we call him Pou,' Nana stated. 'Because he is a pillar of strength.'

Hurahura's feelers stood tall above her head.

'This is my kāinga!' she growled. 'My home! Why are you destroying it?'

Pipi Pouākai flapped her wings and hovered above the centipede.

'We are not here to destroy,' she declared. 'We're here to tautoko and to awhi.'

The myriapod's antennae stretched out towards her.

'First it was the two-legged,' Hurahura continued. 'Then it was the four-legged, and now it is you. This has been my kāinga for over two hundred years. I will not let you hurt the great kauri, our matua. He is father to many.'

'Auē, e te rangatira,' Nana sighed, resting her hands atop her tokotoko. 'I feel your mamae. It is that hurt that has brought us here. We have come to ensure that you and the great matua Tīkokekoke are left in peace.'

Whitu

Hurahura reached out with her antennae and gently touched Nana's face. The tohunga stood still, allowing the connection.

'A rāhui has been placed on this ngahere,' she informed the centipede. 'It is to protect Tīkokekoke, and all of his tamariki and mokopuna whāngai, tamariki whāngai and mokopuna. No one is supposed to be visiting this forest.'

Hurahura tilted her head.

'Many of the two-legged have stopped coming here,' she advised. 'But there is still some that turn up and they bring many four-legged with them. They leave the four-legged to grow and multiply. The four-legged trample on great matua's roots, dig up the soil, rub off his bark and spread disease. They do this to the entire wao, the ngahere.'

Pipi Pouākai flew down and landed beside her grandmother.

'What would the four-legged be, Nan?' she queried.

'They are not native,' hissed Hurahura. 'I have eaten a lot of them.' Salvia dripped from her jaws. 'They're tasty; however, I can't keep up with the numbers. There're just too many. If they are not stopped they will kill Tīkokekoke and this forest.'

69

Pou te Taniwha remained atop Hurahura, pressed flat against her back and listening to the conversation.

'Can I hop off now?' he called out.

Nana noticed Pipi Pouākai's feathers ruffling slightly.

'Pipi, can you feel that draft?' she asked.

The eagle raised her head and felt the air. 'Āe.'

'You need to locate its source,' Nana directed. 'It will lead you out of the cave. Once you are above ground, I want you to fly over the forest and see if you can find these four-legged creatures that Hurahura speaks of.'

'Hello!' chimed Pou te Taniwha. 'Yoo-hoo, can anyone hear me?'

Nana reached up and gently took two

glow-worms from the cave wall and placed them on either side of Pipi Pouākai's beak.

'Here, these can be your headlights,' she chuckled. 'That way you can see where you are going in the dark tunnels. I don't want you hitting your head.'

'She needs a horn too,' quipped Pou te Taniwha.

He wasn't enjoying being ignored.

The eagle's eyes went from Nana to the giant centipede with venom-dripping pincers, and back again.

'Are you sure I should leave you?' she questioned, worried for her grandmother's welfare.

'Pou and I have got this,' Nana reassured her.

Pipi Pouākai beat her wings, lifted off the

ground, and flew over Hurahura, through the cave, and off into one of the tunnels out of sight.

The tohunga pushed her glasses up on her nose.

'Tama, you can let Hurahura go now,' she instructed.

'Yah, finally!' the taniwha exhaled, thankful that Nana was paying attention to him. He was about to let go when doubt crept in. 'Now, she did try and eat me. Is it safe to release her?'

Nana nodded. 'She has felt our intentions.'

Warily, Pou te Taniwha softened his hold and climbed down the side of the gigantic centipede. He stepped around the front of the myriapod, giving the jaws and the forcipule claws a wide berth.

'No biting!' he ordered, pointing at Hurahura who had turned to him.

She twitched her venomous pincers, making him jump.

'Hey!' he shouted, lifting his hands at the ready and backing up behind his grandmother.

The centipede laughed. 'Aroha mai, sorry, I couldn't help myself. I find it exhilarating when my food panics.'

Pou te Taniwha gulped. 'Nan?'

The tohunga sat down on a rock on the cave floor. Her fingers ran over the grooves of her moko kauae.

'Once I know what these four-legged creatures are I will know how to fix it,' she thought aloud.

Feeling something touch his shoulder, the

taniwha flashed a quick peek to his rear. It was one of Hurahura's long antennae. Low to the floor it had snuck around and come up behind him. He faced off with the centipede.

'You're trying to distract me so that you can eat me,' he snapped.

'E, taniwha, you are too much fun,' Hurahura snorted. 'But I'm not going to harm you. We are kaitiaki, both guardians and protectors.'

Pou te Taniwha lowered his hands and looked the centipede over. He still wasn't sure that he could trust her. Her yellow legs were softly lifting up and down like fingers tapping on a tabletop.

'Man, you're big,' he remarked, taking in her colossal size. 'How many legs do you have? 98? 106?'

75

'One hundred exactly,' answered Hurahura.

'Kāo, that's not possible,' spouted the taniwha. 'While the name centipede actually means 100-footed, no centipede can have exactly one hundred legs. You fellas only ever have an odd number of pairs, such as fifteen or twenty-five. You can't have an even number like fifty.'

'Oh, you are a joy,' Hurahura laughed with her head in the air. 'I'm impressed with your knowledge of my kind, Pou. Thank you for telling me what I can and cannot have.' Her antennae waved about like hands as she spoke. 'But tell me, if my body has fifty-one segments, which it has, how many legs is that?'

Pou te Taniwha took a moment to count on his fingers. 'A hundred and two,' he boasted, quite pleased with himself not only for his maths but also for being right and proving his point.

'And if I were to lose a couple?' the centipede's tail came over the top to reveal a pair of legs missing from one segment and the scars of cuts along the end of her body.

'Whoa, what happened?' gaped the taniwha, impressed as much as he was concerned by the wounds.

'I had a disagreement with a large katipō named, Kaiwhatu Kōrehu,' replied Hurahura. 'Mist Weaver.'

'Who won?'

'Let's just say that in the end, we agreed to disagree,' she said. 'Don't worry, my legs will grow back. Us myriapods are clever like that. As of right now though, I am exactly one hundred footed.'

'That must have been some battle,' Pou te Taniwha commented. 'I know if I was going in a cage fight, I'd want to be you, especially with all that weaponry you have. The sharp pointed hooks on each leg, the strong exoskeleton, the sharp jaws for piercing and tearing, and then there're those scary as black-tipped, poisonous daggers you call claws.' He shook at the sight of them.

Hurahura bowed her head slightly.

'E, Taniwha, tēnā koe,' she said. 'To be honest, though, the last thing I'm interested in is doing battle. I am here to protect and look after Tīkokekoke and this ngahere.'

Waru

With a glowing titiwai attached to either side of her beak, Pipi Pouākai cautiously navigated her flight through the dark tunnel, tracking the flow of air back to its source. At times she had to drop down to avoid juts in the roof, in other parts she went high to clear rocks and mounds. There was even a point where, with her wide wing span, she had to angle her body to fly through a narrow gap. Every now and then she would pass scratching sounds, and wonder if it were rats, bats, or wētā scurrying around in the black.

Soon the eagle saw daylight. It was just a faint dot in the distance to begin with, however, the closer she got the larger it grew.

'At last,' chirped Pipi Pouākai as she emerged from the mouth of a cave in the ngahere.

She manoeuvred carefully in and out of the trees and soared into the air above the forest. The shine of Tamanuiterā warmed her wings and the breath of Tāwhiri-mātea, the father of the wind, blew her feathers, ridding her of the dark and cold that she had experienced in the tunnel.

'This is more like it,' she sighed, relieved to be back in her element, high in the sky. Underground is no place for a giant bird of prey.

'Pouākai, titiro atu ō whatu!' Pipi Pouākai cried, and with an eagle eye, she studied the land below, searching for the four-legged that Hurahura had spoken about.

The forest was dense and it was hard for the raptor to penetrate the thick foliage with her glare. Raising her view, she observed the vast reach of the ngahere.

'This is going to take forever,' she moaned.

She caught sight of a pair of kererū, flying low, a short distance from her. Thinking the local bush pigeons may have knowledge of any unusual visitors to the area, she banked, by lowering her right wing while raising her left, and headed towards them.

Pipi Pouākai was able to get close behind the birds without them noticing. She noted

the metallic green and copper feathers of the
kererū reflecting the sunlight.

'Yo, what's up my homies!' she squawked.
'Have you seen any four-legged?'

With a quick tilt of their heads, the much
smaller kererū saw the giant predator swooping
down towards them. Their eyes popping,
the two pigeons pulled their wings into their
bodies, pointed their beaks to the ground, and
plummeted from the sky into the treetops.

Pipi Pouākai chased after them.

'Taihoa, I'm not going to eat you!' she cried.
'Honest, I'm not a threat!'

Kererū are agile for darting through the trees
in the ngahere; however, there wasn't enough
space for the enormous wings of the giant
eagle to fly like that, even if she was still just a
juvenile.

83

The only way for Pipi Pouākai to keep up with the pair was to stay above the forest. She could hear the whooshing sounds of their beating wings, as they went under and over the branches of the different rākau beneath her.

'Seriously, I won't harm you!' she promised. 'I'm looking for the four-legged. Do you know what they are?'

The kererū swept over a small opening in the trees where Pipi Pouākai spotted a line of motley-coloured animals walking one behind the other.

'Goats,' the raptor muttered. 'The four-legged are goats.'

Pipi Pouākai looked at the kererū.

'Tēnā korua!' she squawked. 'Thank you, my friends, it would have taken me ages to find them without your help!'

The pigeons fluttered off into the bush.

Pipi Pouākai circled around getting another look at the hoofed and horned mammals. Now that the eagle knew what it was that she was searching for, she was confident that she could find more if they were there. She flew on, her eyes scanning the forest. It wasn't long before she located another group through the treetops, but it wasn't goats this time.

'Pigs,' the raptor uttered.

The black, feral hogs were bunched together, grunting while grubbing in the ground with their upturned tusks.

Pipi Pouākai spread her wings and glided to the edge of the forest.

'Uh, that's cute,' she remarked when she came across a third collection of animals. 'Deer.'

The mob of reddish brown does and fawns were grazing on the lower leaves hanging from a tree.

A roar caught Pipi Pouākai's attention. Standing tall on a nearby hill was a large stag with huge antlers. Pointing his head skyward the adult male grunted loudly, proclaiming his dominance over the land.

'Try roaring like that around Hurahura,' the eagle thought aloud. 'Then you'll know who's ruler of this ngahere.'

Pipi Pouākai had flown quite a distance, yet it wasn't hard for her to find the way back. Not when she could see Tīkokekoke rising high above all the other rākau. She knew that the cave wasn't far from the great kauri.

During her return flight, the eagle passed over even more herds of goats, pigs, and deer.

When she reached the opening to the tunnel, she found Hurahura crawling out with Nana and Pou te Taniwha sitting on her back. Pipi Pouākai slowly flew in between the trees and around the branches to land in front of the gigantic centipede.

'Huri hei kōtiro!' she cried, transforming into a girl.

The tips of Hurahura's antennae reached out to Pipi and gently explored her face.

'You young ones are clever with your shape-shifting,' she remarked.

'What did you find?' Nana asked, peering over the top of her glasses with a cracked lens.

The girl gave a full report.

Nana shook her head. 'I thought it would be game. Some hunters release animals into the native bush so they can hunt them. Those introduced species can do a lot of damage to our forests.'

'There are heaps of them,' informed Pipi. 'It would take us weeks to find and catch every single one.'

Hurahura used her yellow legs to assist the tohunga in climbing down from her back.

'E te rangatira, I have an idea,' Nana announced, addressing the myriapod. 'It would mean that for a few days, the ngahere will be loud and busy, but after that, it would return to being quiet and peaceful.'

Hurahura stretched her antennae out towards Tikokekoke, and Nana realised that the myriapod was using the feelers to communicate with the kauri. The centipede's attention soon came back to her.

'We are trusting you, Nan,' Hurahura said.

Iwa

Nana stood in the middle of a ngahere with her grandchildren, Pipi and Pou te Taniwha.

'Huri hei tama! ' Pou te taniwha cried, turning into a boy.

Hurahura traversed his face with her antennae, examining his change.

'That tickles,' Pou giggled.

'Wow, your cousin's a pouākai, you're a taniwha,' Hurahura commented. 'What does your grandmother change into?'

'She can be a taniwha too sometimes,' Pou replied cheekily.

'Oi, that's enough of that,' huffed Nana. She took her phone from her kete and handed it to him. 'You kids know how to work the device better than I do. Phone PM in my contacts for me please, boy. An audio call, not a video. We don't want her seeing Hurahura in the background.'

Pou frowned as his fingers tapped away. 'PM? Who's that?'

'Prime minister,' Pipi answered smugly.

She couldn't understand why Nana hadn't given her the phone. She would have found the number much quicker than Pou.

'You've got Prime Minister Reihana's private number in your contact list?' the boy smirked. 'Awesome.'

'Why, are you going to propose to her in a text message?' joked Pipi. 'Or should that be, ask her for a babysitter?'

'Whoa, are you still holding onto that?' Pou chuckled. 'Let it go already.'

He had located the name PM, clicked on it and now passed the mobile back to his grandmother while sneering at Pipi.

Nana put the mobile to her ear.

'Let's hope I've got good reception this time,' she remarked, recalling her climb onto the roof of her whare.

'I can help with that,' Hurahura volunteered, waving her long antennae in the air. 'I have the best aerials around. I pick up lots of radio stations. There are some awesome wonderful tunes on there. Country music is my favourite though.'

The giant centipede wrapped the end of one feeler around Nana's arm holding the cell phone, while her other feeler pointed straight up at the sky.

'It's ringing,' Nana smiled, impressed with the increased clarity of the device.

Pou sat on the ground beneath the fronds of a nīkau palm. Pipi noticed her cousin watching Hurahura's black-tipped, venomous claws and stood next to him.

'They're scary, eh?' she said, quietly.

'I'm just glad that she's on our side,' he breathed.

'Kia ora, Reihana,' sang Nana, turning on the speaker phone.

'Are you back home already, Nan?' the minister asked.

Her voice on the other end of the call was coming through loud enough for everyone to hear.

'Kāo, we're still in the forest,' Nana answered.

'But your phone reception? It is so clear,' Minister Reihana laughed, obviously remembering the gymnastics at her visit.

Nana reached over the forcipule claws and patted Hurahura's face with her free hand.

'Āe, I'm getting some help with that,' she chuckled. 'Hey, we've found the source of the problem. There's a whole lot of goats, pigs, and deer here. The ngahere is overrun with pests.'

Minister Reihana giggled and sighed. 'Those silly scientists and police. They must have mistaken the animals for some sort of monster,'

'Hmm,' Nana looked at the gigantic fanged centipede. 'An easy mistake I guess.'

'Well, it's simple enough to fix,' the minister continued. 'I'll inform the local park rangers and they can address the issue.'

Nana thought for a moment.

'It might be too much for the rangers,' she commented. 'Probably take them forever with their limited personnel, time, and resources. I liked your idea about using the armed forces yesterday.'

Minister Reihana coughed. 'A bit overboard, don't you think? Sending in the army, air force, and navy just to collect some animals?'

Nana nodded. 'Āe, girl, you have such clever solutions, and the number of animals is quite high. It would be a great training exercise for our troops, and they've got those fancy thermal cameras that pick up heat, and helicopters to move people in and stock out, so the job could be done in no time.'

'Oh, Nan, I'm really not sure...' the minister started to say before Nana cut her off.

'Imagine the headlines in the media. The voters would certainly be impressed. I can hear them now, "Look at how serious Prime Minister Reihana is about protecting our environment." And "Our prime minister really cares about our sacred and special kauri." And "Isn't it great how she utilises our armed forces for the welfare of Aotearoa."'

The phone was quiet.

Nana started to wave a finger about in front of her face as she continued her argument.

'You have told me how hard it is to get things done in parliament; to get law changes approved and passed,' she said. 'And people complain about the empty promises of politicians. They wouldn't be able to say that this time though, would they? The proof of the successful capturing of the animals would be there for all to see within a week. It's a win–win.'

There was another moment of silence as the tohunga waited for the prime minister to respond.

'That sort of news could go all around the world,' Prime Minister Reihana reflected out loud. 'It would be an impressive accomplishment for my term as leader.'

'One of many, I'm sure,' added Nana.

'I'm going to do it,' the minister said after a pause. 'I'll make the calls right now.'

'You go, girl,' Nana beamed. 'Lead the way.'

It was late afternoon when a large, grey NH90 helicopter arrived with a whup–whup–whup over the treetops. The crew aboard had used modern technology to track Nana's phone. After spotting the grandmother and her moko waving from amongst the flora below, the pilot landed in a nearby clearing.

Nana looked behind her as she, Pipi and Pou made their way to the aircraft. She was happy to see that Huruhuru was nowhere in sight.

Pou nudged Pipi and gestured at the helicopter with its rotor blades slowing down.

'Ho, I hope they give us a fly in that thing,' he grinned. 'How cool would that be?'

Pipi flapped her arms.

'So cool,' she said sarcastically.

'Not all of us can fly, you know,' Pou scowled.

'Tēnā koutou,' greeted the captain aboard the chopper. 'I understand that we have a pest problem?'

'Āe, tika,' replied Nana. She eyed the leader and his crew of four. 'It's an invasion and you're going to need more troops.'

'We're just reconnaissance,' the captain explained. 'Here to survey the area. The rest of the forces are arriving tomorrow.' He held out a hand to the whānau. 'You want to show us what we're looking for?'

'Oh,' Nana gulped. 'Okay.'

She allowed the captain to help her climb into the helicopter.

'Ka mau te wehi!' Pou cheered with his fists in the air. 'Awesome! We're gonna fly.'

Pipi rolled her eyes. Taking to the sky was nothing new for her.

The rotor blades started to turn above the craft. Nana and her moko were shown to their seats, strapped in, and fitted with headsets so that they could hear and talk to one another over the loud engine.

As the helicopter lifted off and rose into the air, Pipi couldn't help but laugh at her cousin. His excitement had faded and he was now looking worried. Pou wasn't used to heights.

'Whatever,' he grumbled through his headset at Pipi. 'I'd like to see you deep underwater. That's my element.'

Nana and Pipi directed the chopper over the forest, showing the crew the locations of the hoofed animals out the open side door. One soldier had a map of the ngahere on screen and was marking the areas.

'There they are!' Pipi cried, pointing at a mob of deer galloping through the rākau to get away from the aircraft.

'Right, well we can take it from here,' said the captain. 'Let's get you folks back to your car.'

'Aye, aye, captain!' Pou saluted.

Nana, Pipi, and the crew all looked at him and smiled.

'It's not a pirate ship,' Pipi giggled.

Tekau

As Nana had foretold, the forest was very busy over the next few days. The armed forces were fully committed to the mission and used all of their manpower and technology to locate and capture every goat, pig and deer.

The troops fanned out in separate manoeuvres, tracking and corralling the animals or busily building temporary roads so that large trucks could load them up and move them out of the bush. Overhead, the helicopters first helped to track hooved animals in the more difficult areas, and then, using huge nets dangling from beneath them, they transported the livestock to yards that had been constructed near the main road at the edge of the ngahere.

They even caught possums, feral cats, stoats, ferrets and rats. The introduced animals were relocated to farms or were found homes with enthusiasts who offered to help.

The armed services didn't see any sign of Hurahura though. The giant centipede remained hidden beneath Tīkokekoke. There were no reports of a scary monster this time. Eventually, after the army, navy, and air force had completed their assignments, the forest was deemed pest and predator free and the soldiers moved on to repair any damage they had caused to the forest floor, and then plant young saplings to help rebuild the ngahere.

Throughout the operation Prime Minister Reihana featured in news articles and on talk shows around the world, telling of the commitment of her government to protecting the natural environment and of all the work that was being done. She vowed to ensure that the protection and care of the kauri and the ngahere would be maintained. The media reported that her popularity as a leader in Aotearoa had grown as a result of this exercise.

When all was quiet and the armed forces had returned to their bases, Nana and her moko visited the forest again. Tīkokekoke was already looking more vibrant. Hurahura crawled down from the summit of the tree. The whānau watched the gigantic centipede circle around the trunk on her one hundred legs all the way to the bottom, where she greeted them with a bow of her head.

'E te rangatira, tēnā koe, we've come to spend the afternoon with you,' Nana announced. 'And I've been baking.'

She presented the myriapod with a picnic of cheese scones and a flask of hot tea.

'Last year's batch,' Nana announced, holding up a jar of her Blackberry Jam.

'Nan's the best baker,' Pipi stated.

Pou was quick to climb up on Hurahura's back, with her approval of course. The last thing he wanted to do was to upset her and get close to those forcipule pincers again. He was planning to stay as far away from the venomous fangs as possible, and where better than right behind them.

'Kei te pēhea koe?' queried Nana. 'How are you, Hurahura? How is the ngahere now that the animals have gone?'

The centipede raised the front of her body and reached out to the bush with her antennae. She was so big that she had forgotten that Pou was on top of her exoskeleton. He was left dangling from one of her segments, much to Pipi's amusement.

'A warning would have been nice,' Pou groaned, hanging on with both hands.

'Ah, Nan, if it hadn't been for you and your moko the wao would have been overrun with the four-legged,' Hurahura answered, obviously greatly relieved. 'Already the forest is beginning to recover. It will take time, but at least now Tīkokekoke's forest can breathe again, and so can I.'

She lowered her body to the ground and her feelers gently caressed the tohunga's face.

'Humans are tenacious. What is to stop them from returning and repeating the same mistakes?'

A relieved Pou had scrambled back to his original position on the myriapod's back.

Nana gently stroked Hurahura's antennae with her hand.

'For now, Prime Minister Reihana is determined to see this area protected,' she uttered. 'And my moko and I will be supporting and encouraging other guardians to care for Tīkokekoke and the ngahere. We'll be keeping

an eye on things. After all, we are kaitiaki. It is what we do.'

'I just hope it's enough,' hissed Hurahura, her poisonous pincers opening and closing.

Pipi placed her hands on her hips and looked up at the great kauri towering over them.

'We could have been famous, Nan,' she sighed. 'We could have been in those news articles with the prime minister. She did ask us to be in them.'

Nana took a deep breath as she gazed at the forest around her.

'Kāo, we are humble people,' she said, patting the side of Hurahura. 'Only the quiet ones get to see wonders like this.'

'Well, as long as Pou gets to see Prime Minister Reihana sometime soon,' Pipi jested. 'Eh, cous?'

Pou stood tall on top of Hurahura. He stuck out his lips and gave a cheeky overconfident grin, while simultaneously flicking his head and brow in reply.

'Chur,' he said.

Nana laughed. 'Keep dreaming, tama.'

Glossary

āe – Yes

aiii – oh no!

Aotearoa – Māori name for New Zealand

aroha mai – sorry

ata mārie – good morning

auē – heck! oh dear!

awhi – to embrace

e – a term of address

haka – fierce rhythmical dance

haere mai – come, welcome

he aha – what?

hika mā – for goodness sake!

hongi – to press noses in greeting

huia – an extinct species of wattlebird from Aotearoa

hura – giant centipede

Huri hei kōtiro – the command Pipi uses to transform from an eagle into a girl.

Huri hei tama – the command Pou uses to transform from a taniwha into a boy.

iwa – nine

ka pai – good

ka mau te wehi! – awesome!

ka rawe – excellent

kai – food

kāinga – home

kaitiaki – guardian/custodian

kāo – no

karanga – formal call

katipō – species of spider native to Aotearoa

kaumātua – elder/elders

kauri – species of tree native to Aotearoa

kei te pēhea koe – how are you?

kererū – species of pigeon native to Aotearoa

kete – basket

kia kaha – be strong, keep going

Kia ora – hello/cheers

kia pai mai hoki! – wow, that's fantastic!

Kōauau pongāihu – a small gourd nose flute

koru – spiral motif

kōtiro – girl

kuia – elderly woman/women

kura – school

mahi – work

mamae – hurt

manuhiri – visitor

matua – father

moko – grandchild/grandchildren

mokopuna – grandchild/grandchildren

moko kauae – traditional chin tattoo

mōrena – good morning

ngahere – forest

nīkau – a palm tree endemic to Aotearoa

nono – backside

ono – six

pouākai – an extinct species of giant eagle from Aotearoa

Pouākai, haere mai – the command Pipi uses to transform into an eagle

pūkana – to stare wildly, dilate the eyes

rāhui – embargo, traditional ban

rākau – tree/trees

rangatira – chief, noble, esteemed, revered

rima – five

rongoā – traditional medicine

rua – two

tahi – one

taihoa – wait, hold up

tama – boy

Tamanuiterā – personification and sacred name of the sun

tamariki – children

taniwha – monster

Tāwhiri–mātea – Father of the wind

tautoko – to support

tekau – ten

tēnā koe – hello to one and a way to say thank you.

tēnā korua – hello to two

tēnā koutou – hello to three or more

te reo Māori – the Māori language

tika – correct, right

titiro mai – to look

titiwai – glowworms

tohunga – expert

tokotoko – carved walking stick

toru – three

wahine toa – warrior woman

waiata – song/sing

waka – vehicle

wao – forest

wētā – insect species native to Aotearoa

whā – four

whakarongo – to listen

whānau – family

whāngai – adopted

whare – house

whitu – seven

Character's names:

Hurahura – big cenitipede

Tīkokekoke – to be high in the heavens

Kaiwhatu kōrehu – Mist Weaver

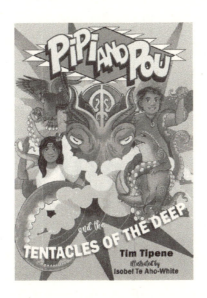

If you enjoyed this adventure with Pipi and Pou and their Nan, then try reading another story in the series.

Pipi and Pou and the Tentacles of the Deep

9781990035289

Nan insists on a day at the beach with the whanau but there is something strange about the dangerous rip she can see from the shore.

pipiandpou.com

The first chapter of Pipi and Pou and the Tentacles of the Deep

Tahi

Nana's old car coughed and spluttered, blowing bubbles of waiata and aroha from the exhaust, as it pulled up at a beach, under a row of Christmas coloured pōhutukawa. Nana's waka, Betsy, didn't run on petrol or power. It ran on songs and love.

'Here we are,' the tohunga smiled beneath her sunglasses.

Pipi was sitting next to her in the front passenger seat.

'Good thing you found a park,' she said, gesturing at all the other vehicles lining the side of the road.

Nana's hands rested on the steering wheel. She eyed the golden sand, the blue sea, and the white foam-crested waves rolling into shore.

'Ātaahua, what a beautiful day,' she uttered, momentarily lost in the bliss of her surroundings. She turned to her moko. 'Make sure you two have got plenty of sunscreen on. It's gonna be a hot one.'

'Already done, Nan,' Pipi replied, showing the residue of grease on her hands leftover from applying the cream.

Pou pulled the latch and pushed the back door open with his foot. His eyes scanned the many people dotted in groups along the shore.

The first chapter of Pipi and Pou and the Tentacles of the Deep

'They're here,' he announced, spotting members of their whānau together on the beach. The relatives were gathered on and around woven flax mats which had been spread out on the sand.

Pipi climbed out of the car. 'Cool, Uncle Hēmi brought his guitar.'

'You can show him how to play it, girl,' Nana chuckled, standing on the grass and donning her apricot-coloured, straw sun hat which was adorned with flowers.

Nana and her moko took bags and kai from the back of the waka and carried them down onto the beach to join their whanaunga.

'Kia ora, Nan!' everyone sang when she neared.

'Tēnā koutou,' Nana beamed. The

grandmother loved nothing better than to be with family and to see all her other mokopuna. She gave everyone a hongi, a kiss on the cheek, and a hug.

Pipi and Pou did the same. Then they ran to the water with their cousins.

Nana leaned on her tokotoko, watching the waves and smelling the sea breeze.

'Ahh, this is the life,' she breathed.

'You can relax now, Nan,' said Aunty Kaia, who was standing nearby tying up a little girl's hair.

'Āe,' Nana nodded. She sat down on one of the woven mats and watched Pipi and Pou play with their relatives in the shallows. Tamanuiterā, the sun, was shining bright and there wasn't a cloud in the sky. It was a perfect

The first chapter of Pipi and Pou and the Tentacles of the Deep

day for the beach, yet as much as she tried
Nana couldn't relax. She turned to see an old
man standing on the grass under a bright red
and green pōhutukawa. He was watching her.
Nana had first noticed the elder hanging around
when she had been unpacking her car.

'Kei te pēhea koe, Nan?' Aunty Kaia asked,
sitting down and taking hold of her hand. 'How
have you been?'

The tohunga smiled at the middle-aged
woman.

'Kei te pai, dear,' she answered. 'You know
me. I like to keep busy.'

'Still driving all over the motu I hear?'
muttered Aunty Kaia, shaking her head. 'Forever
trying to better the world, eh? We would be lost
without you.'

Nana was renowned for attending different hui at marae up and down the country, and for supporting and offering āwhina to her people.

'It's not just me,' stated Nana. 'I'm slack compared to other kuia. Do you know that I missed two meetings last week because I was busy doing other things?'

'Really?' said Aunty Kaia, raising her brow and knowing full well that the old woman was never one to accept any praise or recognition.

Nana looked back at the grass, but only saw a flock of tarāpunga, red-billed seagulls, squabbling over bits of discarded food. She noticed that the old man had gone.